Mission: Space Science

Chasing Comets, Asteroids, and Mysterious Space Objects

Nancy Dickmann

CRABTREE
PUBLISHING COMPANY
WWW.CRABTREEBOOKS.COM

Mission: Space Science

Author: Nancy Dickmann

Editors: Sarah Eason, Tim Cooke, Ellen Rodger

Editorial director: Kathy Middleton

Design: Paul Myerscough, Lynne Lennon

Cover design: Paul Myerscough

Photo research: Rachel Blount

Proofreader and indexer: Jen Sanderson, Wendy Scavuzzo

Production coordinator and prepress technician: Ken Wright

Print coordinator: Katherine Berti

Consultant: David Hawksett

Produced for Crabtree Publishing by Calcium Creative

Photo Credits:
t=Top, tr=Top Right, tl=Top Left

Inside: ESA: ESA / Rosetta / MPS for OSIRIS Team MPS / UPD / LAM / IAA / SSO / INTA / UPM / DASP / IDA: p. 17; ESO: ESO / M. Kornmesser: p. 38; NASA: pp. 10, 31, 32, 33; NASA / Ames: p. 11b; NASA Goddard Space Flight Center Image by Reto Stöckli: p. 18; NASA / Johns Hopkins University Applied Physics Laboratory / Southwest Research Institute: p. 35; NASA / JPL: p. 11t; NASA / JPL-Caltech / Arizona State Univ. / Space Systems Loral / Peter Rubin: p. 27; NASA / JPL-Caltech / UCLA / MPS / DLR / IDA: pp. 6, 25; NASA / JPL / UMD: p. 13; NASA / JPL / UMD / Pat Rawlings: p. 12; SOFIA / Lynette Cook: p. 4; Alan Stern (Southwest Research Institute), Marc Buie (Lowell Observatory), NASA and ESA: p. 40; Phys.org: NASA / Dimitri Gerondidakis: p. 7; Shutterstock: 3Dsculptor: pp. 45t, 45b; Edobric: p. 44; Industry And Travel: p. 29; Jan Kaliciak: p. 8; Markusenes: p. 30; Roman Mikhailiuk: p. 28; Muratart: p. 5; SUWIT NGAOKAEW: p. 42; ProStockStudio: p. 43; Turtix: p. 9; Space.com: NASA, ESA, and G. Bacon (STScI): p. 37; Wikimedia Commons: CSIRO: p. 39; DLR: pp. 16, 23t; ESA–C. Carreau / ATG medialab: pp. 1, 14; ESA / Rosetta / NAVCAM: p. 15; Go Miyazaki: p. 22; NASA: pp. 19, 23b, 24, 26; NASA / Johns Hopkins University Applied Physics Laboratory / Southwest Research Institute: p 34; NASA / JHU APL / SwRI / Steve Gribben: p. 36; NASA / JPL: p. 21; NASA / MSFC / David Higginbotham / Emmett Given: p. 41; Gregory H. Revera, NASA / JPL-Caltech / UCLA / MPS / DLR / IDA: p. 20.

Cover: Wikimedia Commons: State Farm.

Library and Archives Canada Cataloguing in Publication

Dickmann, Nancy, author
Chasing comets, asteroids, and mysterious space objects / Nancy Dickmann.

(Mission: space science)
Includes index.
Issued in print and electronic formats.
ISBN 978-0-7787-5392-6 (hardcover).--
ISBN 978-0-7787-5398-8 (softcover).--
ISBN 978-1-4271-2207-0 (HTML)

1. Comets--Juvenile literature. 2. Asteroids--Juvenile literature. 3. Near-Earth objects--Juvenile literature. I. Title.

QB721.5.D53 2019 j523.6 C2018-906104-9
C2018-906105-7

Library of Congress Cataloging-in-Publication Data

Names: Dickmann, Nancy, author.
Title: Chasing comets, asteroids, and mysterious space objects / Nancy Dickmann.
Description: New York, New York : Crabtree Publishing, [2019] | Series: Mission: Space science | Includes index.
Identifiers: LCCN 2018050346 (print) | LCCN 2018052347 (ebook) | ISBN 9781427122070 (Electronic) | ISBN 9780778753926 (hardcover) | ISBN 9780778753988 (pbk.)
Subjects: LCSH: Comets--Juvenile literature. | Asteroids--Juvenile literature. | Near-Earth objects--Juvenile literature.
Classification: LCC QB721.5 (ebook) | LCC QB721.5 .D53 2019 (print) | DDC 523--dc23
LC record available at https://lccn.loc.gov/2018050346

Crabtree Publishing Company
www.crabtreebooks.com 1-800-387-7650

Printed in the U.S.A./032019/CG20190118

Published in Canada
Crabtree Publishing
616 Welland Ave.
St. Catharines, Ontario
L2M 5V6

Published in the United States
Crabtree Publishing
PMB 59051
350 Fifth Avenue, 59th Floor
New York, New York 10118

Published in the United Kingdom
Crabtree Publishing
Maritime House
Basin Road North, Hove
BN41 1WR

Published in Australia
Crabtree Publishing
Unit 3 – 5
Currumbin Court
Capalaba QLD 4157

Contents

CHAPTER 1

What Are Comets and Asteroids?

Earth is part of a **solar system** made up of objects that **orbit** the Sun. These objects include eight **planets** (Earth is one of them) and millions of smaller objects. Some travel close to the Sun, while others stay in the outer reaches of our Solar System, far from the Sun. Many of these small objects are asteroids and comets.

Asteroids

Asteroids are small lumps of rock and metals scarred with **craters**. The largest is 329 miles (530 km) across, but others are the size of a house or smaller. So far, about 780,000 asteroids have been identified, but there are many more. Most asteroids lie in a "belt" between the orbits of Mars and Jupiter.

Asteroids dislodged from the asteroid belt travel through our Solar System on paths that sometimes bring them close to planets.

A comet's "tail" is a stream of dust and gas extending away from the comet as it travels around the Sun.

The asteroid belt contains millions of asteroids. Other asteroids, called **Trojans**, share an orbit with a planet. Many Trojans share Jupiter's orbit, and one shares Earth's orbit! Other asteroids travel close to Earth's orbit.

Comets

Comets are also small and lumpy, but they contain ice and dust as well as rock. Most comets come from the outer edges of our Solar System. They travel around the Sun in a long, looping path. As they approach the Sun, they warm up and some of their ice turns into a gas. The gas forms an **atmosphere** called a **coma**, which can reach out into a long "tail." Comets often become visible to the naked eye when they pass close to Earth. Some comets appear regularly. Halley's Comet, for example, is visible about once every 76 years. Other comets take millions of years to complete their journey around the Sun.

New Discoveries

Comets and asteroids are small and difficult to reach, but that has not kept **astronomers** from studying them. The information astronomers have gathered has helped them understand more about the beginning of our Solar System—and the early days of our own planet, Earth.

Why Study Comets and Asteroids?

No astronauts have ever visited a comet or an asteroid, but in recent decades astronomers have sent many spacecraft to study them. Astronomers also use powerful **telescopes** to learn more about comets and asteroids. Telescopes on Earth are often built on mountains and in deserts, where the air is clear. Other telescopes are in orbit above Earth's atmosphere, where the view of space is clearer still.

Comets streaking across the sky have fascinated people for thousands of years. Ancient peoples saw them as **omens**, or signs, that warned of disasters to come. It was only natural for people to try to learn more about these **phenomena**. Asteroids, on the other hand, are smaller and only rarely come close enough to be visible from Earth. For that reason, they were not even discovered until 1801.

Scientists use telescopes to monitor asteroids, such as this one, and their journeys through space.

In the Beginning...

About 4.6 billion years ago, our Solar System was nothing more than a cloud of dust and gas. At some point, the cloud collapsed in on itself, forming a disk. Most of the dust and gas came together and formed a star, the Sun. The rest remained in orbit around the new star. Tiny pieces collided and clumped together, forming larger and larger objects. Some of these lumps eventually became planets.

Asteroids and comets are some of the leftovers of this planet-forming process. They never became part of a planet. By studying them, scientists can learn about our early Solar System. Asteroids and comets may help us understand why the eight planets of our Solar System are so different from each other. They may also explain how life began on Earth, and whether it might exist on other planets.

Scientists have built many special space probes to visit and study asteroids and comets.

Types of Asteroids

Astronomers divide asteroids into three types, based on what they are made of. C-type asteroids are the most common and are made of clay and rock. S-type asteroids are made of rock and metal, and M-type asteroids are mainly metallic. Astronomers use different tools to study the **composition**, or makeup, of asteroids. A few asteroids have been studied closely by visiting spacecraft, called **probes**. These probes use tools called **spectrometers** to analyze what asteroids are made of. Scientists study other asteroids using spectrometers on ground-based telescopes. They also use **radar**, by sending a radio signal to the asteroid and studying what is reflected.

Using Asteroids

One reason that astronomers and **entrepreneurs** find asteroids fascinating is because the rocks are packed with **natural resources**, such as metals. Planetary Resources is a company figuring out ways to **mine** asteroids. It has identified one asteroid less than a mile across that could contain more of the precious metal **platinum** than has ever been mined on Earth. Mining asteroids would be difficult and expensive—but the results could be incredible.

In addition to minerals, asteroids and comets also contain water. Access to drinkable water is an issue for many people on Earth, and the problem is likely to become worse. Just as water is essential for life on Earth, it will be just as vital for humans exploring the Solar System.

Space Colonies?

Science fiction books and movies sometimes show humans setting up **colonies** on asteroids or other planets. Earth faces many challenges, such as climate change, so it might one day become a good idea to set up colonies in space. Human miners may work on asteroids in the future, but setting up a permanent colony would be extremely difficult. However, the resources found on asteroids—minerals, water, and more—could be useful for supplying future space colonies on Mars or the Moon. In 2017, the China National Space Administration (CNSA) announced plans to build a mining base on an asteroid.

Spacecraft may one day carry robots that will mine valuable resources from asteroids.

Incoming Asteroid!

Every day, about 100 tons (91 metric tons) of space material lands on Earth in the form of dust or small **meteorites**. It causes little damage. However, larger objects occasionally hit the planet. For example, a massive asteroid impact about 65 million years ago probably helped wipe out the dinosaurs. Other impacts formed large craters that can still be seen on Earth's surface.

The **gravity** of larger objects in space, such as planets, can sometimes nudge an asteroid out of its normal orbit around the Sun and onto a slightly different path. Some of these asteroids come scarily close to Earth! These are known as near-Earth asteroids. Studying as many of them as possible helps astronomers predict where they will go. With enough warning, we may be able to prevent a future impact.

Meteor Crater in Arizona is 0.75 miles (1.2 km) across. It was formed by a meteor impact about 50,000 years ago.

CHAPTER 2

Chasing Comets

Comets can be tricky to study. Although distant comets can be spotted with telescopes, they must be closer to Earth to be visited by a spacecraft. Even then, they are moving targets! Comets speed up as they approach the Sun. Near Earth, they can be traveling at tens of thousands of miles per hour.

Halley's Comet

In 1705, the British astronomer Edmond Halley suggested that comets observed in 1531, 1607, and 1682 were actually the same comet, making return journeys. He predicted the comet would be seen again in 1758. Fifty-three years later, he was proven right!

The comet passed close to Earth again in 1986. It was greeted by a fleet of five spacecraft, called the "Halley Armada." One of them, Giotto, was sent by the European Space Agency (ESA). It came within 370 miles (596 km) of the comet's nucleus and sent back more than 2,000 photos.

Some spacecraft, such as Stardust (above), are designed to capture material from comets.

Giotto showed that the body of the comet was dark and peanut-shaped, and about 9 miles (15 km) long. The comet was also 80 percent water.

Comet Dust

The Halley Armada revealed new information about comets, but there was still more to learn. In 1999, the U.S. National Aeronautics and Space Administration (NASA) launched an ambitious mission called Stardust. Its goal was to capture dust from a comet's tail and return it to Earth. In 2004, Stardust passed through the tail of Comet Wild 2. A device called a collector grid captured thousands of **particles**, or tiny pieces.

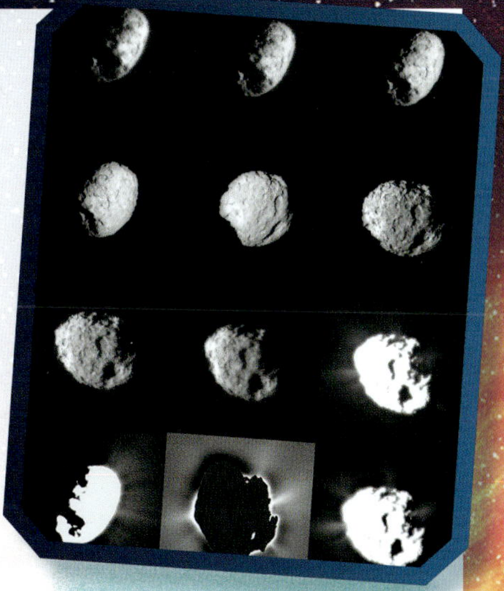

Stardust took a series of images of Comet Wild 2.

MISSION:

Space Science

Scientists analyzing the material collected by Stardust found that the dust in the comet dated back to the earliest days of our Solar System. They also found an **amino acid** called glycine. Amino acids are chemicals that make up proteins, the building blocks of life. Could a comet have delivered amino acids to Earth, leading to the development of life? If comets have delivered amino acids elsewhere in our Solar System, might life form there, too?

The Deep Impact spacecraft carried a list of 625,000 people who applied to send their names to a comet.

Comet Collision

Nearly all of the particles that Stardust brought back to Earth came from the surface of Comet Wild 2. They had been released as the comet moved closer to the Sun. The comet warmed up and its ice turned into gas. To find out more about the inside of a comet's center—its **nucleus**—scientists built a new spacecraft named Deep Impact. It was designed to crash into a comet.

The idea was simple, but the mission required complicated engineering and navigation to succeed. The spacecraft was in two parts: a **flyby** spacecraft and an **impactor**, the part that would crash into the comet. The impactor weighed 820 pounds (372 kg) and was made mostly of copper and aluminum. Deep Impact also had equipment onboard that helped it adjust its course.

Impact!

Deep Impact launched in January 2005 and took six months to reach its target—Comet Tempel 1. Once it was close enough, the spacecraft released the impactor into the comet's path. It crashed into the comet, creating a deep crater. The flyby spacecraft stayed close so it could analyze the pieces of rock thrown out by the impact.

Deep Impact carried scientific instruments with equipment that could detect carbon **molecules**. It also carried a spectrometer. It would look for water, carbon monoxide, and carbon dioxide.

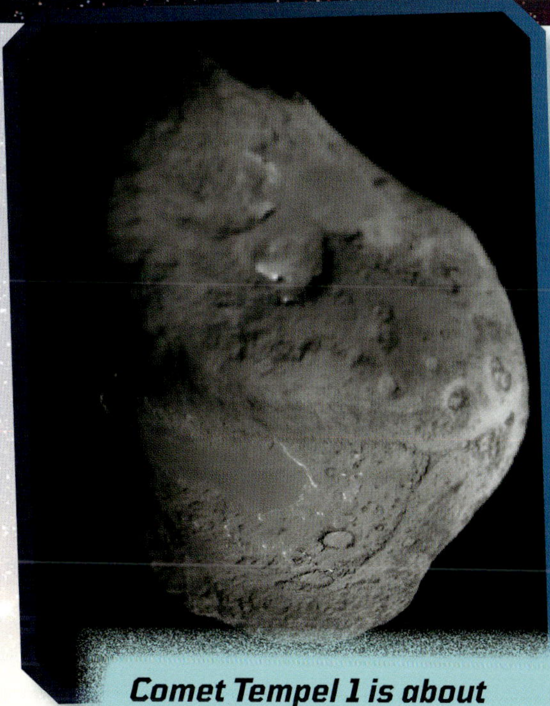

Comet Tempel 1 is about 3.75 miles (6 km) across. It orbits the Sun every six years.

Successful Mission

After its encounter with Comet Tempel 1, Deep Impact flew past another comet, named Hartley 2. It used its instruments to study this second comet even though it had already used the impactor. The spacecraft provided several important discoveries. It showed that a comet's surface is very **porous**, or has a lot of holes. At least 75 percent of the outer 32 feet (10 m) or so of the nucleus is empty space. Deep Impact also found evidence that some comets formed closer to the Sun than others.

YOUR MISSION

Although the impactor from Deep Impact collided with Comet Tempel 1 at high speed, the crater it formed was only about 100 feet (30 m) deep. If you wanted to analyze material from deeper inside the comet, how might you go about it? Think about possible solutions, such as drilling or using radar from an **orbiter**. Which would be easiest on a fast-moving comet?

Rosetta

There is a limit to how much a spacecraft can learn by making a flyby. To study a comet in depth, a spacecraft needs to enter orbit around the comet. The Rosetta spacecraft made history by doing just that. After years of planning, Rosetta launched in 2004. It took a 10-year journey to reach its target, a comet known as Comet 67P/ Churyumov-Gerasimenko.

Comet 67P was heading toward the Sun when Rosetta went into orbit around it in August 2014. The spacecraft stayed in orbit around the comet as it looped around the Sun and started on its journey back to the outer Solar System. In September 2016, with its job completed, mission organizers steered Rosetta to crash directly into the comet's nucleus.

Rosetta traveled with Comet 67P for two years before crashing into the comet's nucleus.

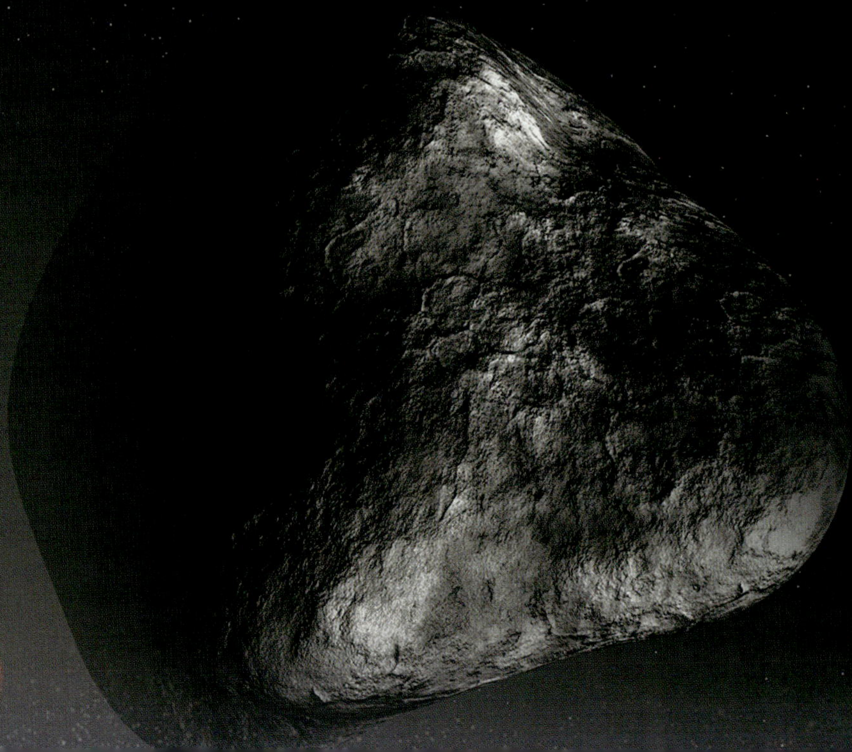

Rather than being a ball-shaped lump, Rosetta found that Comet 67P looks a little like a rubber duck!

Comet 67P

Comet 67P originally came from the Kuiper Belt, a band of icy objects beyond the orbit of Neptune. At some point, it was dislodged from its orbit and tossed toward the Sun. It now orbits the Sun every six-and-a-half years.

There were several reasons why astronomers chose Comet 67P as Rosetta's target. They wanted a comet that was fairly active and had already made several trips around the Sun. The comet needed to have a flat orbit, in line with the disk formed by the orbits of the planets around the Sun. Comet 67P met all three of these requirements. It also had an orbit that would put it in the right place at the right time.

MISSION:

Space Science

Rosetta's scientific instruments revealed a lot of information about the comet. They measured its size and showed that it was made up of clumps of ice and dust. Rosetta also found that the comet's dusty surface helped control its temperature and protect the ice beneath. Cracks on the comet's surface are likely caused by the cycle of heating and cooling that happens as its orbit brings it closer to or farther from the Sun.

Philae

By going into orbit around a comet, Rosetta gave scientists a chance to study the comet in depth. However, it did even more. It released a smaller spacecraft, called Philae, which became the first human-made object to successfully land on a comet.

Planning a Landing

Once Rosetta was close enough to Comet 67P, scientists used its data to choose a landing site. The comet was becoming more active as it moved closer to the Sun. Scientists needed to find a location that would be safe to land in but also **exposed**, or not hidden, enough to allow Philae's **solar panels** to charge its batteries through sunlight.

Comet 67P is so small that gravity on the surface is very weak. There was a real risk that the box-shaped **lander** might hit the surface and bounce back off into space. To avoid this, engineers attached **harpoons**, or spearlike parts, and ice screws to Philae's three legs. They were designed to fix the lander to the surface as soon as it touched down.

Philae carried solar panels that would turn sunlight into the electricity needed to power the lander's instruments.

Crash-Landing!

However, when Philae landed on Comet 67P on November 12, 2014, the harpoons did not fire. The lander bounced about half a mile (1 km) into the air and ended up tipped sideways on a cliff face. Worse, it had landed in the shadow of the rocks. No sunlight reached its solar panels. It was only able to communicate with Rosetta for a few days before its batteries died.

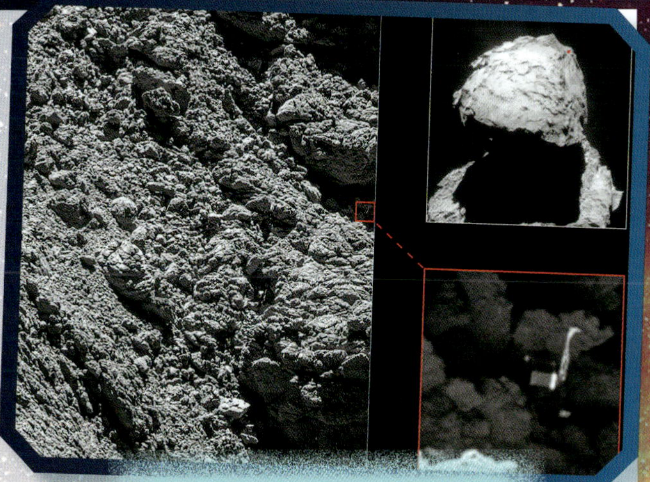

Philae ended up hidden away in a rocky cliff (bottom right).

In the short time before its batteries died, Philae discovered a lot about the comet. The lander's gas-sniffing instruments identified the gases present on the surface. They also detected chemical **compounds** containing carbon and nitrogen. Some of these compounds help form amino acids. Amino acids had not been found on a comet before. Rosetta helped study the inside of the comet by sending radio waves through it, which Philae picked up. The waves showed that there is more ice than dust, with a lot of empty space in between.

YOUR MISSION

Engineers on the Rosetta mission had to think creatively when Philae did not land where they wanted it to. It proved impossible to move the probe before its batteries died. How do you think they might have gone about learning as much about the comet as possible within the short time they had?

Comets and Earth

Every discovery from spacecraft such as Deep Impact and Rosetta adds to our knowledge. Slowly but surely, astronomers are building up a picture of how Earth formed and changed over many billions of years.

Comets might help solve one mystery—where the oceans came from. No other planet has surface water like Earth. Could it have been present when Earth formed, or did it arrive later?

Viewed from space, Earth has so much water it has been nicknamed a "blue marble."

For many years, some astronomers thought that icy comets crashing into Earth brought water with them. However, Rosetta found that water vapor from Comet 67P has a different chemical composition from water on Earth. Studies of other comets gave similar results. Many astronomers now think that Earth's water must have come from asteroids instead.

What's Next?

A lot still remains to be learned about comets. CAESAR is a mission proposed by NASA astronomers. ("CAESAR" stands for Comet Astrobiology Exploration SAmple Return.) If the mission goes ahead, CAESAR will eventually pay another visit to Comet 67P/Churyumov-Gerasimenko. Unlike Rosetta, however, it will not go into orbit around the comet. Instead, it will use a robotic arm to scoop up a sample of material from the surface, then return it to Earth.

Answering Questions

Combined with the information from Rosetta—which astronomers are still analyzing—the sample from CAESAR could help answer many questions about comets. By studying the chemical makeup of the comet's material, scientists hope to learn more about the compounds that form the raw materials of life. They will compare the samples from Comet 67P with samples of space dust collected on Earth. They hope to get a clearer picture of how comets may have brought life to Earth.

MISSION: Space Science

Even after a mission finishes, there are still discoveries to be made. Scientists spent years analyzing the samples brought to Earth by the Stardust spacecraft in 2006. In 2014, they announced that seven tiny grains of material collected by the probe originally came from outside our Solar System. They are particles of **interstellar dust**—tiny pieces of rock found in the enormous spaces between the stars.

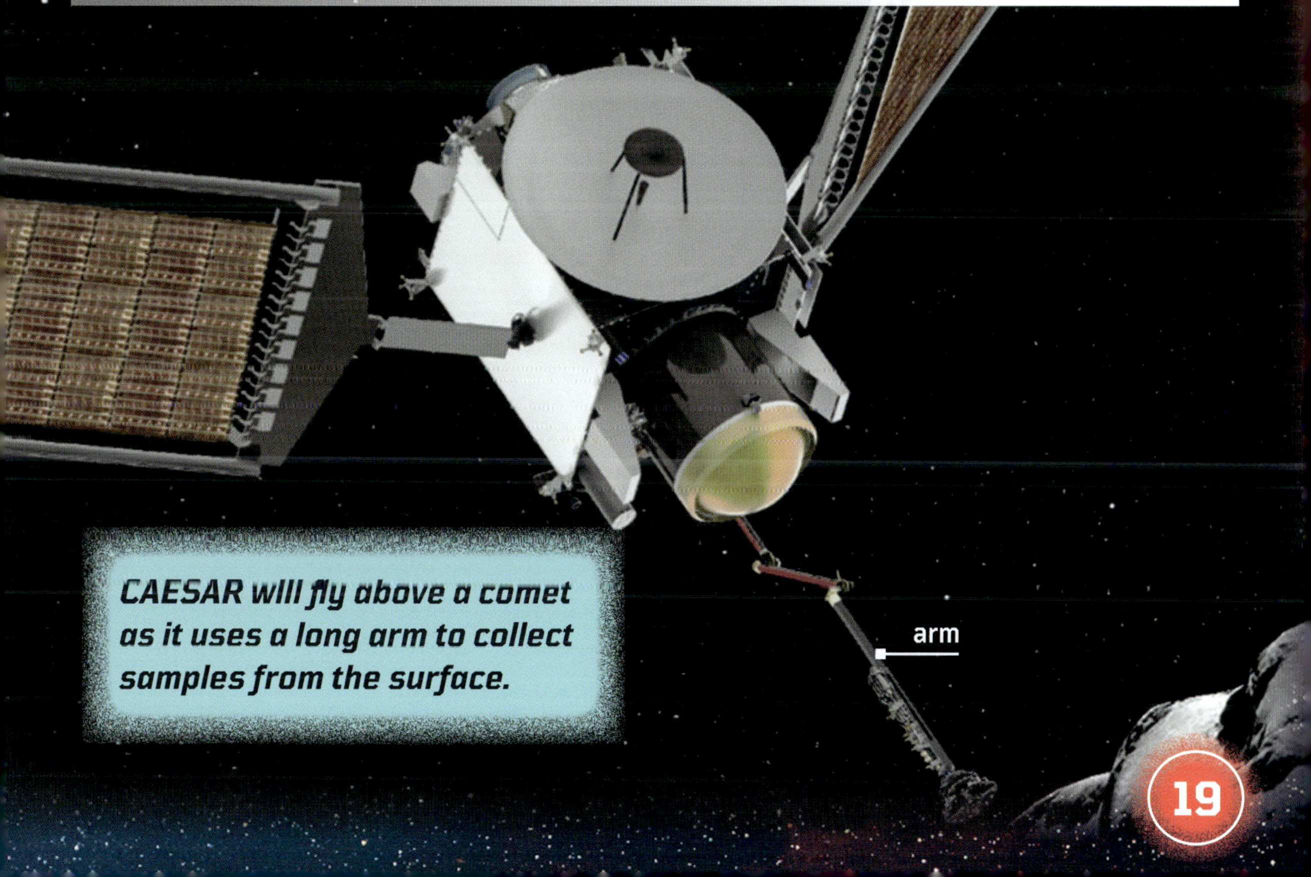

CAESAR will fly above a comet as it uses a long arm to collect samples from the surface.

CHAPTER 3

Visiting Asteroids

With their glowing comas and long tails, comets passing Earth are clearly visible to the naked eye. However, asteroids are small, dim, and far away. This makes them very difficult to spot, even with a telescope.

In the 1700s, the German astronomer Johann Bode found that the distances of the planets from the Sun seemed to follow a mathematical pattern. However, Bode noticed a gap between Mars and Jupiter, where the pattern seemed to show that there should be a planet. Could there be a missing planet still awaiting discovery? Astronomers began to search the skies. In 1801, the Italian astronomer Giuseppe Piazzi made a discovery—but it was not what anyone expected. Rather than finding a missing planet, he had found Ceres—the largest object in the asteroid belt.

This illustration shows the size of Ceres (bottom left) compared to the Moon (top left) and Earth (right).

The asteroid Ida is about 19.5 miles (31.4 km) across. It has its own tiny moon, named Dactyl.

Going In-Depth

Technology in Piazzi's time was not advanced enough for scientists to learn much about asteroids. This remained the case for about 190 years. It was only in 1991 that NASA's Galileo spacecraft flew close enough to an asteroid to send back clear photos.

Galileo was on its mission to Jupiter when its course brought it within 1,000 miles (1,600 km) of the asteroid Gaspra. Galileo's cameras revealed a small, oddly shaped rock with a surface that was scarred with craters. Two years later, Galileo flew past another asteroid, Ida. As it did so, it discovered a tiny moon in orbit around Ida. This was the first discovery that some asteroids had their own moons.

NEAR-Shoemaker

In 2000, NEAR-Shoemaker became the first spacecraft to go into orbit around an asteroid. It studied the asteroid Eros for a year, at one point traveling just 3.3 miles (5.3 km) from the surface—lower than a passenger jet flying above Earth. In 2001, the spacecraft landed on Eros. It transmitted valuable data from the surface for more than two weeks.

The thousands of images sent back by NEAR-Shoemaker revealed 100,000 craters and more than 1 million large boulders. The spacecraft also collected information on the chemicals that make up Eros. This helped scientists understand how asteroids are linked to meteorites found on Earth.

Hayabusa

In 2003, the Japan Aerospace Exploration Agency (JAXA) launched an ambitious asteroid mission. The Hayabusa spacecraft would study the asteroid Itokawa before landing on the surface. After collecting a sample of rock, the spacecraft would return to Earth for scientists to study the material. The spacecraft faced numerous technical problems during its mission, but its control team on the ground was able to overcome them. Hayabusa got the sample safely back to Earth and provided a huge amount of **data** about Itokawa.

Itokawa

Like Eros, Itokawa has an orbit that brings it near Earth. It was discovered in 1998 by researchers studying near-Earth asteroids (NEAs) and named for Hideo Itokawa, a famous Japanese rocket engineer. Itokawa is a very small S-type asteroid, less than half a mile (1 km) long. Because it is so small, its gravity is too weak to hold a spacecraft in orbit around it. Hayabusa had to adjust its own orbit around the Sun to match that of the asteroid until it had "parked" itself in a position about 12 miles (20 km) above the surface.

Hayabusa landed on the surface of Itokawa for about 30 minutes before taking off again.

New Discoveries

Hayabusa revealed that Itokawa is what is called a "rubble pile asteroid." Rather than being a solid object, it is a jumble of rocks that are held together only by their gravity. There are very few craters on the surface. This is because any large impact would shake loose rocks that would then fill up the hole. However, Itokawa was probably once part of a larger object. Some of the dust brought back by Hayabusa shows signs that it was formed inside a larger object.

Hayabusa brought back tiny particles of Itokawa to Earth.

MISSION:

Space Science

The Hayabusa spacecraft used a fairly new technology to travel through space: the **ion engine**. A rocket burns fuel, releasing gases that push the spacecraft in the opposite direction. Fuel is heavy, however, so carrying enough for a long mission is difficult. An ion engine shoots out a stream of tiny electrical particles called ions. Ion engines only provide weak **thrust**, or push, so they are not powerful enough to send a spacecraft into space. In space, however, an ion engine can gradually push the craft to high speeds using very little fuel.

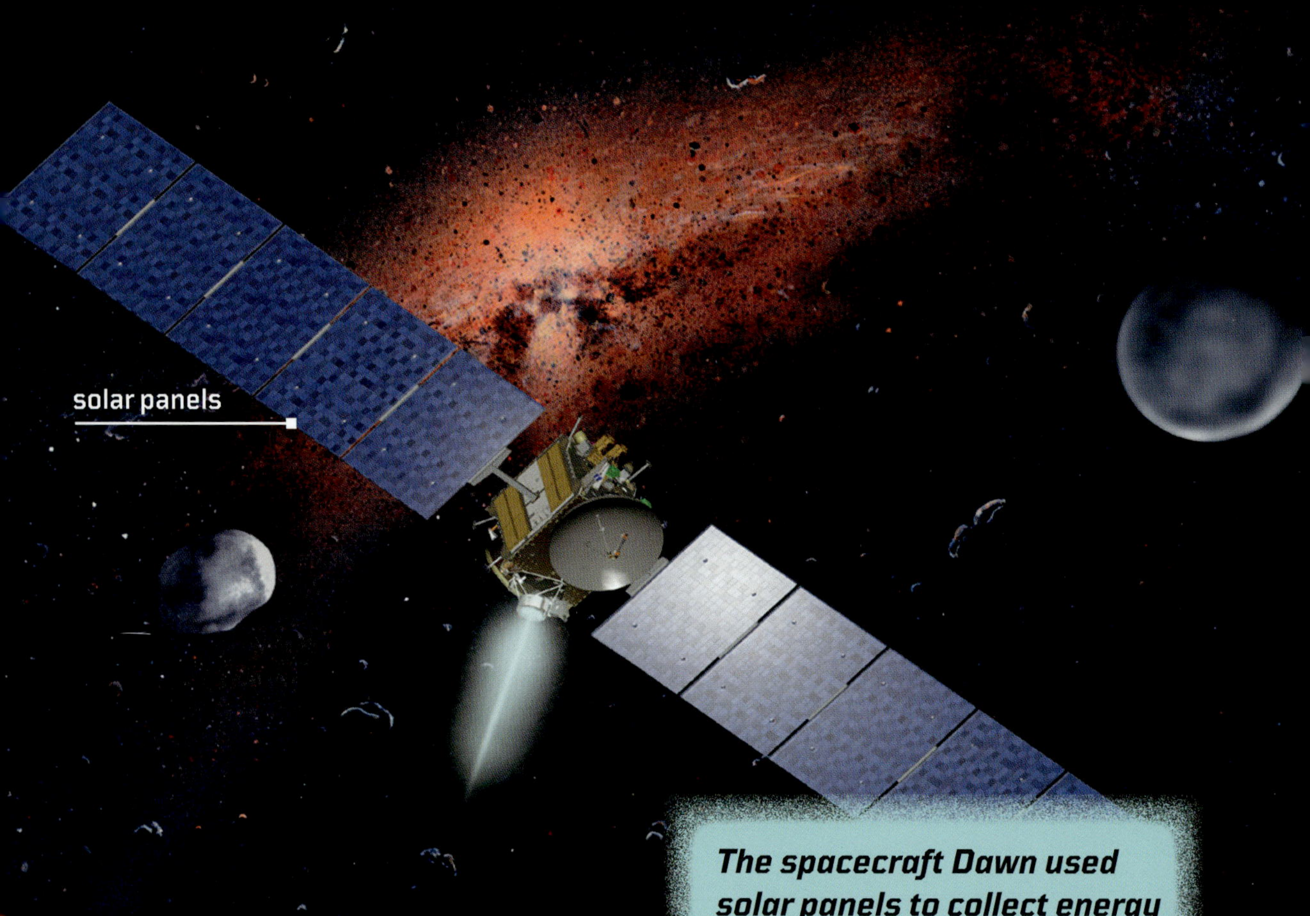

The spacecraft Dawn used solar panels to collect energy to power its instruments.

Protoplanets

A few of the objects in our Solar System are classed as **protoplanets**. A protoplanet is like a baby planet formed from smaller objects that collided and joined together. Unlike most asteroids, protoplanets grow large enough for radioactive material to melt the inside, as it does within planets. Heavier materials sink to the center of the asteroid, forming a layered structure. Vesta and Ceres are two large protoplanets in the asteroid belt.

Dawn

The Dawn spacecraft was designed to visit Ceres and Vesta. Scientists hoped that their state of **arrested development** might provide unique clues about how Earth originally formed. The spacecraft is powered by an ion engine, similar to the one used on Hayabusa. After arriving at Vesta in 2011, Dawn stayed in orbit for more than a year before traveling on to Ceres. It is the first spacecraft ever to orbit two different bodies other than Earth.

Ceres

Ceres was the first asteroid to be discovered, back in 1801. It is the largest body in the wide belt of asteroids that lies between Mars and Jupiter. In 2006, Ceres was placed in a new category that astronomers had just created: **dwarf planets**.

Like the dwarf planet Pluto, Ceres orbits the Sun and is **spherical**, or ball-shaped. This shape is only achieved by bodies that grow relatively large. However, both Ceres and Pluto share their orbits with too many other objects to be true planets.

The Same, but Different

Dawn's data showed that, while Vesta and Ceres may look similar, they are very different. Vesta is smaller and not as round as Ceres. It is mainly rocky, while Ceres has an inner layer made up of frozen water. Some scientists think that Ceres may even have more water than Earth! This ice may be the reason that Ceres has few large craters—over time, ice smooths out any craters. As for Vesta, it lost about 1 percent of its **mass** in a huge collision about 1 billion years ago. As a result of the collision, rocks were thrown into space and some ended up on Earth as meteorites.

Dawn took this photograph of the south pole of Vesta. It shows grooves surrounding the middle of the asteroid.

The OSIRIS-REx spacecraft took off in 2016 and was scheduled to reach the asteroid Bennu in December 2018. It will return a sample of material from the surface. Bennu is a small asteroid, but astronomers are eager to learn more about it. This is because they have been using mathematics to calculate its orbit, and it has a small chance of colliding with Earth at some point in the next 200 years. An asteroid the size of Bennu would create a crater about 4 miles (6.4 km wide). This is smaller than the crater formed by the asteroid that wiped out the dinosaurs, but it would still cause huge devastation on Earth.

OSIRIS-REx will search for Trojan asteroids in Earth's orbit during its voyage to the asteroid Bennu.

Hayabusa2

JAXA's Hayabusa2 spacecraft reached the asteroid Ryugu on June 27, 2018. Ryugu is another near-Earth asteroid that could one day collide with our planet. It is a C-type asteroid, while Itokawa, which was visited by the first Hayabusa, was an S-type asteroid. Hayabusa2 will study the asteroid for a year and a half before returning to Earth with a sample. It will also release three small rovers that will land and "hop" over the surface to study the asteroid. Hayabusa2 carried a small impactor like the one that Deep Impact used to collide with a comet. The spacecraft was intended to study the impact and bring back debris from inside the crater it created.

In the Future

Two more asteroid missions have been proposed, but had not been launched by late 2018. Lucy is a NASA mission that will take a 12-year trip to visit Trojan asteroids near Jupiter. It will be the first spacecraft to study these types of asteroids. Another NASA mission will study Psyche, an unusual asteroid in the asteroid belt. Scientists think Psyche may be the exposed metal **core** (center) of a protoplanet.

YOUR MISSION

The engineers who designed Hayabusa2 tried to improve on the design of the first Hayabusa. Imagine that you were designing a spacecraft to visit an asteroid. What might you want to learn about the target? What would be the best tools for finding out: an orbiter, a lander, or a sample return mission? Give reasons for your answers.

A spacecraft uses its solar panels as it approaches the asteroid Psyche in this artist's impression.

CHAPTER 4

Avoiding Impacts

Sending spacecraft to study asteroids helps scientists learn what they are made of, and helps predict their paths more accurately. This is especially important for NEAs. If scientists discover an asteroid on a path to collide with Earth, they will need plenty of time to plan what to do about it. However, there are too many NEAs for it to be possible to visit them all. Instead, astronomers use telescopes on Earth to find and track NEAs that might threaten Earth.

Finding NEAs

Through a telescope, an NEA appears as a small point of light. In a single photograph, it is impossible to tell one apart from a distant star or **galaxy**. However, in two photographs taken a few minutes apart, stars and galaxies will appear in the same position but an NEA will have moved slightly. By comparing photographs, astronomers can spot NEAs. If they have a long enough series of photographs, they can estimate how fast the asteroid is traveling and how close it is to Earth.

With the naked eye, it is almost impossible to pick out NEAs from among the millions of other lights in the night sky!

Observatories in Hawaii stand on a mountaintop above the clouds.

Asteroid Spotters

Astronomers estimate that there are about 1,000 NEAs more than 0.6 miles (1 km) across and about 15,000 that are larger than 460 feet (140 m). That is big enough to cause significant damage on Earth. NASA plans to discover 90 percent of these asteroids. Its search programs have found and tracked tens of thousands of asteroids.

The Pan-STARRS program is based in Haleakalā, Hawaii. It consists of two telescopes that look for asteroids and comets as well as distant stars. The first telescope contains a digital camera that was the biggest in the world in 2008, when it went into operation. The second telescope's camera is even bigger!

MISSION:

Space Science

Near-Earth Asteroid Tracking (NEAT) was a long-running NASA program that ended in 2007. One of its key instruments was a military telescope in Hawaii. The telescope was originally designed to track spacecraft and other artificial objects orbiting Earth. The Lincoln Near-Earth Asteroid Research (LINEAR) project also used a military telescope. It discovered more than 140,000 objects, including several comets.

An asteroid begins to break up in the atmosphere as it streaks toward Earth.

Avoiding an Impact

If an asteroid is found on a path that will collide with Earth, it must be stopped. In some science fiction movies, astronauts use nuclear bombs to blow up such threatening objects. It may not be necessary to destroy an asteroid, however. Attaching a thruster to push the asteroid off course might stop a collision. A few scientists around the world are working on techniques that might one day save Earth.

Asteroids are all different, so a solution that works for one asteroid may not work for another. The bigger an asteroid is, the more effort will be required to push it off course. Asteroids that are loose piles of rubble might break apart if a mission tried to push them in a new direction, for example. An asteroid that was spinning very quickly would make it difficult to attach a thruster to steer it away from Earth.

Tractors, Impactors, and Mirrors

Among the solutions to deal with different types of asteroids is a plan to send a very heavy spacecraft to meet an incoming asteroid. The spacecraft's weak gravity would gradually pull the asteroid onto a path that would not collide with Earth. This kind of spacecraft is known as a "gravity tractor." This technique could work for any type of asteroid, no matter how fast it is spinning. However, the spacecraft might have to fly alongside the asteroid for many years for its gravity to have an effect. There might not be that much time.

Another solution uses the impact of a moving object to shift an asteroid's course. One or more large spacecraft would ram the asteroid at high speed. The force of their impact might be enough to knock it off course.

Another suggestion is that many small spacecraft could use mirrors to focus sunlight on an asteroid's surface. The heat would turn some of the material into gas. Gas spewing out in one direction would push the asteroid in the opposite direction. A similar idea involves painting an asteroid to change how much sunlight it reflects.

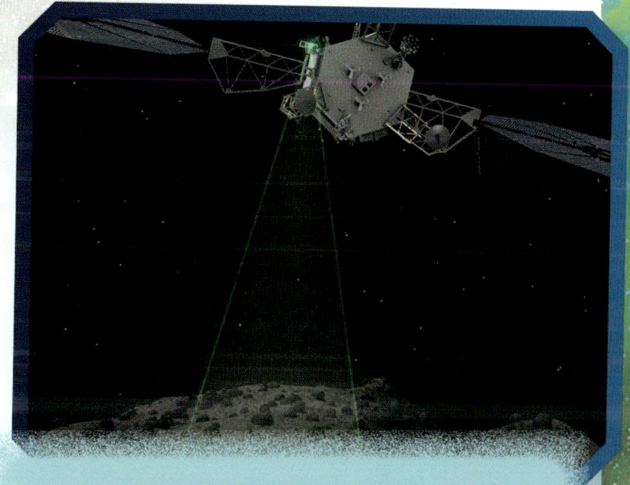

It might be possible to use a mirror to shine sunlight on an asteroid.

YOUR MISSION

Imagine that an asteroid has been spotted heading toward Earth. It is medium-sized, seems to be solid, and it spins slowly. It is due to hit Earth in a year's time. Which of the techniques you have read about would be most likely to change its course?

Capturing an Asteroid

Scientists are not only figuring out ways to deflect asteroids, but they are also planning to capture asteroids, both in order to study them more closely and to access their natural resources. These projects are called "asteroid capture" missions.

Asteroids are sometimes captured naturally, by the gravity of a planet or other large object. If an asteroid just missed Earth, for example, it would not have enough energy to escape the planet's gravity. It would end up in a steady orbit around Earth.

Asteroid Redirect Mission

NASA engineers planned a mission to capture an asteroid with a spacecraft. This Asteroid Redirect Mission would place the asteroid in orbit around the Moon. Once it was in position, astronauts could visit and study it closely. The asteroid might also provide a useful source of water for astronauts staying on the Moon. Water is heavy, so launching it into space is very expensive. Having a much closer source of water would make it easier for astronauts or future settlers to live and work on the Moon.

It may be possible to use a robot to lift a boulder off the surface of an asteroid to place it in orbit around the Moon (see opposite).

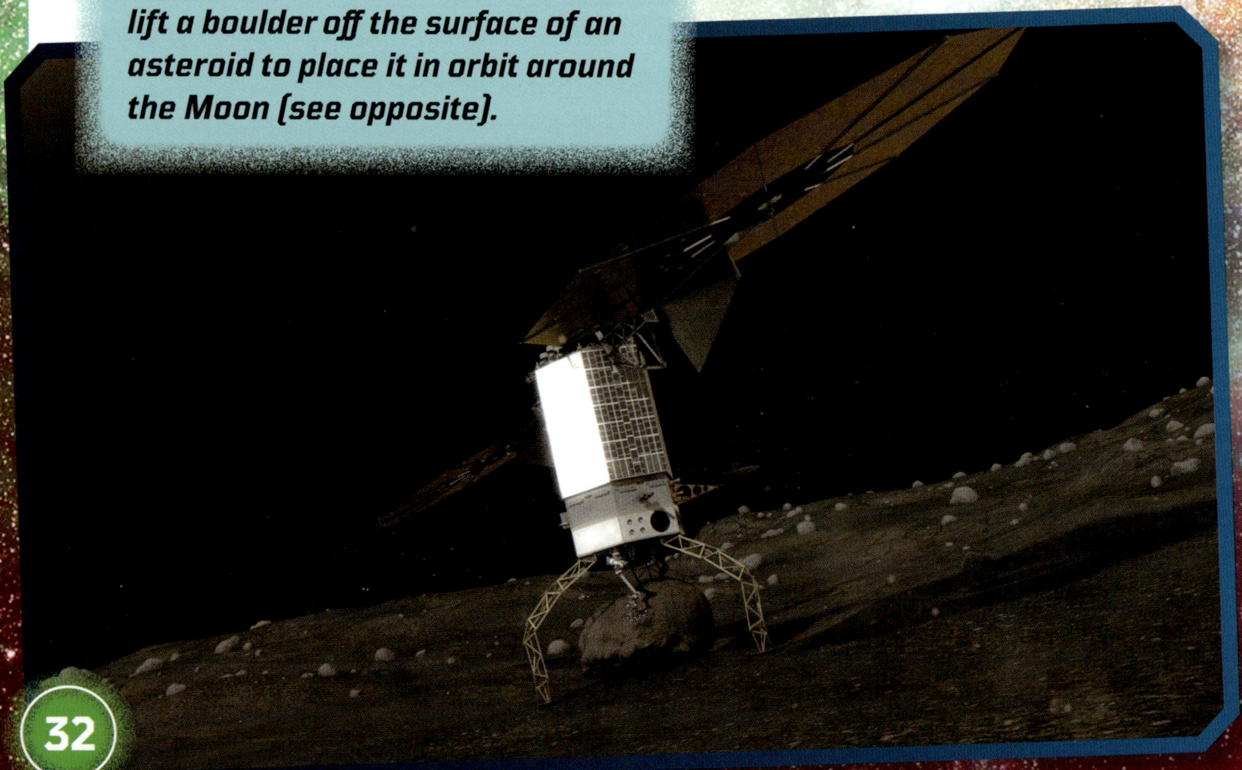

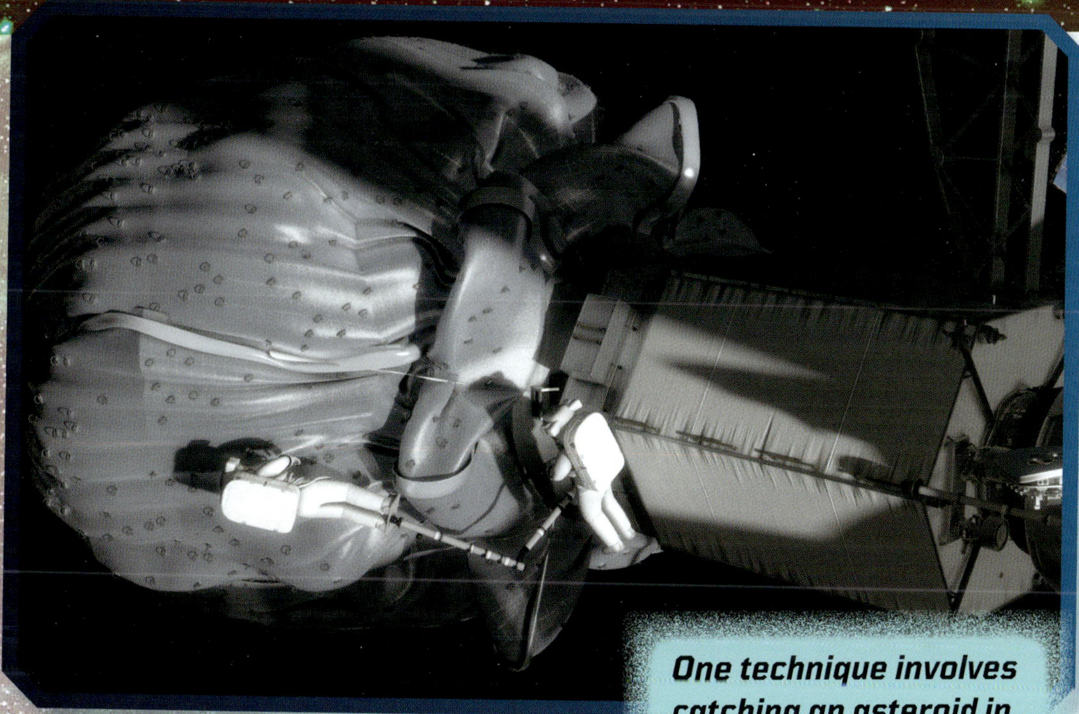

One technique involves catching an asteroid in a large bag.

Testing Methods

One idea for the Asteroid Redirect Mission was for a spacecraft to land on an asteroid and use a robotic grabber to grab a large boulder on the surface. The spacecraft would then take off, pulling the boulder to the Moon to place it in orbit. The journey to the Moon might be an opportunity to test the "gravity tractor" technique for pulling a potentially dangerous asteroid off a direct collision course with Earth.

Another of NASA's ideas was to capture a small, free-flying asteroid, rather than taking a boulder from a larger asteroid. In this technique, a spacecraft would use an inflatable bag like a net to surround and capture the asteroid. The spacecraft would then drag it to the Moon. The mission would take several years to reach the asteroid, capture it, and reach the Moon.

Either of these approaches would have allowed scientists to test out new instruments and spacecraft designs. These innovations could have been useful in other types of space missions. However, the U.S. government canceled the Asteroid Redirect Mission before it was even launched.

CHAPTER 5

Weird and Wonderful

Our Solar System is huge and full of mysteries. The Sun is at the center, orbited by the eight planets—and by many asteroids, too! Beyond Neptune, the farthest planet from the Sun, lies a large doughnut-shaped ring of orbiting objects named the Kuiper Belt. Beyond the Kuiper Belt is a large spherical area called the Oort Cloud, which is filled with small, icy objects. This cloud is the source of some of the comets whose orbits bring them periodically to loop around the Sun.

Pluto

Until 2006, textbooks said that our Solar System had nine planets. The outermost planet was Pluto, a small, rocky world beyond Neptune. Pluto is so small and so far away that even the most powerful telescopes showed it as a fuzzy blob. In January 2006, the New Horizons mission began a 10-year journey to become the first spacecraft to visit Pluto. Before it could get there, however, Pluto was **demoted** into a different category: the dwarf planets.

The first detailed images of the dwarf planet Pluto were not taken until 2015, when it was visited by the NASA probe New Horizons.

New Horizons studied Charon, one of Pluto's moons. Some astronomers think Charon may be a dwarf planet itself.

New Horizons arrived successfully at Pluto in summer 2015. It was not intended to go into orbit around the planet, but it took photographs and other readings as it flew past. The probe gave scientists a huge amount of information about the dwarf planet. Researchers have discovered that a bright, heart-shaped ice formation covers a large part of Pluto's surface. Some of this ice is formed of frozen water, but some is made of nitrogen, carbon monoxide, or methane. On Earth, these substances would be gases, but Pluto is so cold that they are frozen solid. The surface is about -369 °Fahrenheit (-223 °C).

MISSION:

Space Science

Based on all the data sent back by New Horizons, astronomers think that Pluto's moons formed at the same time, billions of years ago. The craters on the moons suggest they probably formed when Pluto collided with another Kuiper Belt Object (KBO). The largest moon, Charon, may have once had an ocean of liquid water beneath the surface. Pluto itself may still hold liquid water. There is also evidence that Pluto may once have had liquid on its surface, as Earth does now.

Other Dwarf Planets

Pluto is only one of the five dwarf planets that are recognized by astronomers. There are three others in the Kuiper Belt. They are Eris, Makemake, and Haumea. Eris is slightly smaller than Pluto, and its discovery in 2005 led to the creation of the "dwarf planet" category. Astronomers felt that if Pluto was a planet, Eris should be, too. They realized that they were likely to find many more objects like Eris. Our Solar System might end up with hundreds of planets, which would be very confusing.

Flying Farther

After leaving Pluto, New Horizons continued into the Kuiper Belt. Its next target is an object called 2014 MU69, which lies about 1 billion miles (1.6 billion km) beyond Pluto. NASA astronomers have given the object the nickname "Ultima Thule," which translates roughly as "beyond the borders of the known world." They believe that it is either peanut-shaped or is perhaps two objects closely orbiting each other. Some clues suggest that it might have its own moon.

New Horizons will be able to solve these mysteries as it performs a flyby of 2014 MU69, getting even closer to the surface than it did to Pluto's.

New Horizons approaches Pluto, with Charon in the distance, in this artist's impression of the mission.

KBOs and Centaurs

New Horizons will not visit any other bodies, but its team hopes to use its long-range sensors to gather data on about 20 other KBOs as it passes. It is also taking measurements of the dust and gas in its path. Only four other spacecraft have ever traveled so far from Earth, so New Horizons will provide important information about what conditions are like.

The spacecraft will also observe objects known as "centaurs." These small bodies may once have been KBOs, but they now have orbits between Jupiter and Neptune. They are like comets in some ways, but like asteroids in other ways. Because of this, they were named for the half-horse, half-human creatures from Greek mythology.

KBOs float in the farthest reaches of our Solar System, from where the Sun appears tiny.

YOUR MISSION

Imagine that you are designing a mission to visit a KBO. What would you like to learn about it? Which instruments would you need to include to get this information? What do you need to know about the object before you launch your spacecraft? Give reasons for your answers.

A Visitor from Another Star

In October 2017, astronomers found the first visitor from outside our Solar System. The object they discovered was not an alien spaceship, although it looked a little like one. Instead, it was an interstellar asteroid, or an asteroid from another solar system. Astronomers named the object 'Oumuamua, which means "a messenger from afar arriving first" in the Hawaiian language.

Mystery Object

When astronomers first spotted 'Oumuamua, they thought it was a comet. However, as the object got closer to the Sun, there was no sign of a comet's usual coma of dust and gas. This showed that the object was likely made of rock or metal, not ice. By studying how its brightness changed, astronomers calculated that it was long and thin—about 10 times as long as it was wide. This is a very unusual shape for a space object, and nothing like it had been discovered before. It is about 1,300 feet (400 m) long and has a reddish color, similar to other objects in the outer Solar System.

'Oumuamua is such an unusual shape that astronomers soon suspected that its origins lay outside our Solar System.

Telescopes in Australia and elsewhere are used to pick up radio waves from space objects.

How Do We Know?

The main clue that 'Oumuamua came from outside our Solar System was its speed. As it looped around the Sun, it was traveling at 196,000 miles per hour (315,430 kph). This is much faster than the speed of a comet. The Sun's gravity alone could not have made the object travel so fast, so astronomers figured out that it must have already been moving very fast when it entered our Solar System. In fact, it is traveling so fast that the Sun's gravity will not be able to stop it leaving our Solar System. It will head back into the Milky Way.

MISSION:

Space Science

'Oumuamua's unusual shape, along with its origin outside our Solar System, led some people to wonder if it might be an alien spaceship. Several different radio telescopes were used to scan for any sort of signals coming from the fast-moving object. If it was carrying alien life forms, they might be sending out messages. However, none of the telescopes found evidence that 'Oumuamua was broadcasting any sort of signal.

CHAPTER 6

What's Next?

At the beginning of the 1900s, astronomers were tracking the orbits of many comets, but they still did not know what the comets were made of. Several hundred asteroids had been discovered, but even with the most powerful telescopes they only appeared as pinpricks of light. Their shape and what they were made of were a total mystery. At the time, astronomers were still in the dark about how these objects formed.

Today, the picture is completely different. Telescopes in orbit around Earth can provide a clearer picture of these faraway objects. Telescopes on the ground have become more powerful and more sensitive. Spacecraft have traveled to comets and asteroids, bringing back samples of their rock to Earth for scientists to analyze.

Before New Horizons visited Pluto, these fuzzy photos, taken by a telescope orbiting Earth, were the best we had.

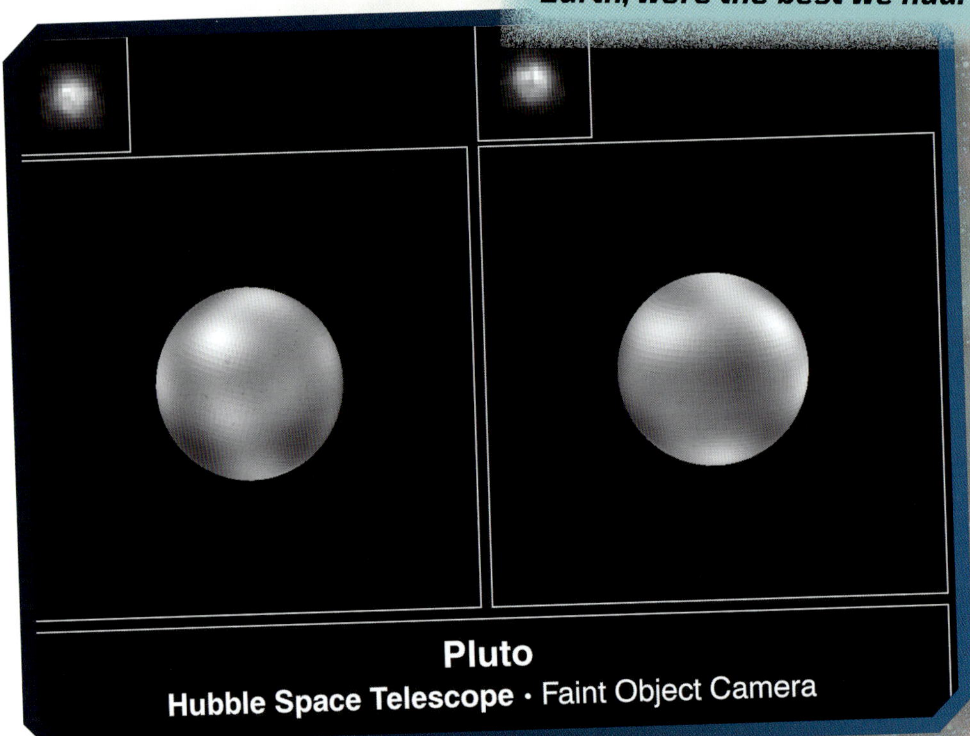

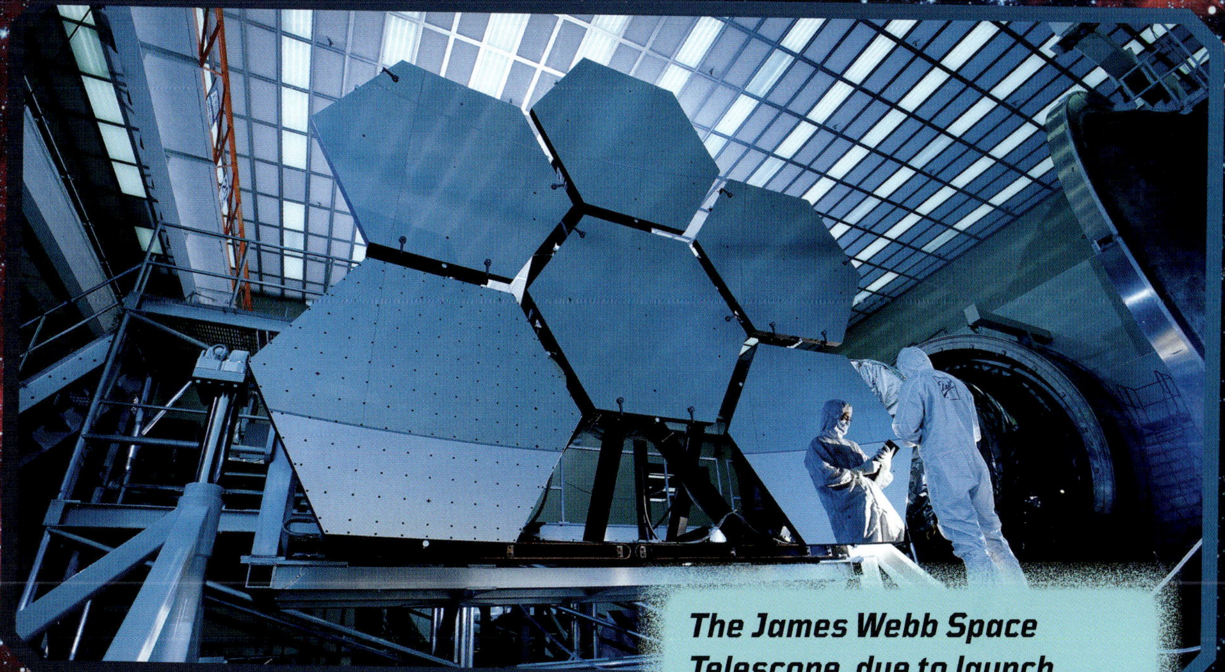

The James Webb Space Telescope, due to launch in 2021, will be the most advanced space telescope yet.

What We Know

Spacecraft that have visited asteroids have brought back valuable data. They have shown that asteroids are rocky, but that some also contain precious metals and frozen water. Scientists have also learned that the largest asteroids have a layered structure, like the planets.

Astronomers know how some asteroids formed, and have been able to tell that certain asteroids are the source of meteorites that land on Earth. Perhaps most important, they have been able to identify and track asteroids that may one day pose a threat to Earth.

Comet Facts

Our understanding of comets has also completely changed. Not so long ago, people still thought they were omens of disaster. Now we know that comets are lumps of ice and rock from the outer Solar System. In 1950, the astronomer Fred Whipple suggested that they were "dirty snowballs" made of ice, dust, and rock. Modern missions have shown he was right. Thanks to spacecraft such as Rosetta and Philae, we have a better understanding of what happens as a comet travels around the Sun and heats up. Scientists have even analyzed the dust of a comet's tail.

More to Learn

Although we have learned a lot about asteroids, comets, and the other small bodies in our Solar System, there is much more to learn. Astronomers still have many questions about how our Solar System formed. They still do not know exactly how life began on Earth, or what will happen to the planet in the distant future. Studying asteroids and comets may provide the answers to some of these questions.

Water World

Earth's water makes it unique: No other planet has liquid water on the surface. But where did the water come from? Some scientists believe it was carried to Earth on asteroids, while others believe it came from comets crashing into the planet. Still others think the water was already here, trapped in rocks, when the planet formed.

Information collected by spacecraft has shown that the water in comets is slightly different from water on Earth, while asteroids contain more water than people had thought. There is still no definitive answer about the origin of water, but future exploration may help us find out for sure.

About 71 percent of Earth's surface is covered in water. Asteroids and comets might hold clues to the water's origin.

Analyzing evidence from space requires a huge amount of effort from scientists working around the world.

Origin of Life

Another question that astronomers would love to answer is how life began on Earth. Were the chemical building blocks always in place here, or did they arrive on Earth from space? When Stardust revealed an amino acid in the tail of Comet Wild 2, that was an important clue. Rosetta then found the same type of amino acid in the atmosphere of Comet 67P, confirming that some comets may contain amino acids. Astronomers hope that further exploration will provide proof that comets are the source of the amino acids that led to life on Earth.

Working Together

Space exploration is a huge challenge. It requires thousands of people from around the world, working together to design new spacecraft and tools. Engineers, computer scientists, chemists, biologists, and many other experts collaborate—all with the same goal of finding out more about the universe. It is difficult work, but it is also very important. Space may provide the resources and discoveries that the human species will one day need to survive. The next big discovery may be just around the corner. Perhaps you will be involved in finding it!

ACTIVITY

Your Space Science Mission

Every year, scientists suggest new missions into space. It can take years to design and build a spacecraft, and even longer for the spacecraft to reach its destination. Space missions take a lot of work—and cost a lot of money. It is important to get things right so the mission has a good chance of success and all that time and money are not wasted.

You have read about some of the remarkable spacecraft that have traveled to the farthest reaches of our Solar System. Now it is your turn to design a mission! Your target can be a comet, asteroid, dwarf planet, or an **interstellar** visitor such as 'Oumuamua. Here are some hints and tips to help get your mission off the ground.

If you could design your own spacecraft, what would it carry? Try drawing an image of how it might appear.

Planning Your Mission

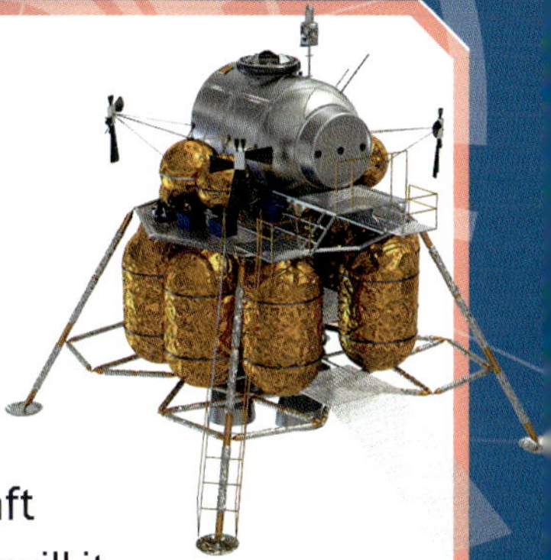

1 Think about what you want to achieve or learn.
Do you want to find sources of water or precious metals in space, for example? Do you want to set up a space colony on an asteroid? Research previous missions to see what has already been learned, and what we still need to find out before we could take such a step.

2 Choose a target.
Telescopes can provide some information about faraway bodies. Try to find one that is not too hard to get to. Remember that scientists have not yet figured out a way to send humans on long missions. If you want to include astronauts in your mission, you will need to choose a destination quite close to Earth.

3 Design your spacecraft.
How will it be powered? If you have a long journey ahead, an ion engine might be best. Research other ideas for powering spacecraft, such as solar sails.

4 Plan how you will gather information.
Will your spacecraft perform a flyby, or will it go into orbit around an asteroid or a comet? Maybe it will release a lander or a rover, or collect rock samples to bring back to Earth.

5 Choose your instruments.
Think about the data you want to gather, and what tools would be best for the purpose. Most spacecraft carry cameras and spectrometers. What other devices might be useful?

6 Collaborate!
Once you have some ideas jotted down, share them with a friend. See if they can come up with suggestions and new ideas to add to yours.

Glossary

Please note: Some **bold-faced** words are defined where they appear in the book.

amino acid A chemical compound that helps to form proteins

arrested development Physical development that is not complete

astronomers People who study objects in space

atmosphere A blanket of gas surrounding a planet or other space object

colonies Settlements established by people from another place

coma A layer of gas that forms around a comet's nucleus

compounds Substances made of two or more different elements

craters Circular holes made when one object hits another in space

data Facts and statistics collected for analysis

demoted Made less important

dwarf planets Bodies that orbit a star but are not large enough to be considered planets

entrepreneurs People who create a business

flyby A flight of a spacecraft close to a space object

galaxy A system of millions or billions of stars

gravity A force that attracts all objects toward one another

interstellar Related to the spaces between stars

lander A spacecraft designed to land on a space object

mass The total amount of material making up something

meteorites Space rocks that land on Earth

mine Extract from the ground

molecules Particles formed from two or more atoms

moon An object that orbits a planet or an asteroid

natural resources Useful materials that occur naturally

orbit The path an object takes around a larger object; or, to take such a path

orbiter A spacecraft that goes into orbit around a space object

phenomena Events that can be observed

planets Large, spherical objects that orbit a star

platinum A dense, silvery precious metal

probes Uncrewed spacecraft

protoplanets Space objects orbiting a star that may develop into planets

radar A system that sends out radio waves and picks them up again

solar panels Panels covered in cells that turn sunlight into electricity

solar system A group of planets that circles a star

spectrometers Devices that can tell what substances something is made of

telescopes Instruments that gather information about distant objects

Trojans Asteroids that share the same orbit as a planet

Learning More

Books

Gifford, Clive. *Astronomy, Astronauts, and Space Exploration* (Watch This Space!). Crabtree Publishing Company, 2015.

Gifford, Clive. *The Solar System, Meteors, and Comets* (Watch This Space!). Crabtree Publishing Company, 2015.

Hamilton, John. *Rosetta: Voyage to a Comet* (Xtreme Spacecraft). A&D Xtreme, 2017.

Jefferis, David. *Space Explorers: From Earth to Infinity* (Our Future in Space). Crabtree Publishing Company, 2018.

Rusch, Elizabeth. *Impact!: Asteroids and the Science of Saving the World* (Scientists in the Field). HMH Books for Young Readers, 2017.

Websites

Want to know more about near-Earth objects and how we track them? Try this website:

https://cneos.jpl.nasa.gov

Find a list of questions and answers about space:

http://coolcosmos.ipac.caltech.edu/asks

This NASA website has everything you need to know about asteroids and other objects in our Solar System:

https://solarsystem.nasa.gov

Go here to find a list of missions to explore our Solar System, both past and present:

www.planetary.org/explore/space-topics/space-missions

Index

About the Author

Nancy Dickmann has written more than 130 nonfiction books for children, specializing in science. Before becoming an author, she worked for many years as an editor and publisher of children's books. She is fascinated by space science and has written many books on the topic.